The Color of My Fur

To all people everywhere.
Let's share the forest in peace.
- Nannette

The Color of My Fur
Text and Illustrations Copyright 2019 by Nannette Brophy Major
ISBN 978-1-7336564-0-5

Published by
Major Masterpieces Ltd.
www.majormasterpieces.com

The Color of My Fur

Nannette Brophy Major

Major Masterpieces Ltd.

Umber was an orange bunny.
He lived in a troubled land.

Three purple bunnies chased Umber to the edge of the forest.
He scurried up a tall mountain and didn't look back until he
reached the top.

"Stay up there!" shouted the purple bunnies as Umber sat breathlessly on the highest ledge. "Keep out of our forest!" they yelled before they disappeared into the trees.

"This is getting worse," Umber gasped.
"I thought the forest belonged to all bunnies."

"So did I," said a strange voice.
Umber looked around but saw no one.
"Who said that?" he asked.

A large, fluffy mist appeared
from behind the mountain.
"I said that. My name is Cloud."

"How do you do, Cloud?
   I am Umber."

"Why were the purple bunnies chasing you?" Cloud asked.

Since Cloud lived high in the sky, he could see everything that happened on the ground.

"There seems to be a lot of fighting in the forest," he added.

"They don't like me because the color of my fur is different from theirs," Umber answered matter-of-factly, as if Cloud should've known this already.

"That's a silly reason for not liking someone,"
Cloud said with a frown. "You're all bunnies."

"I know, but we don't look the same!"
Umber argued, jumping to his feet.

"You all have long ears and cottony tails,"
Cloud continued.

"I guess that's true, Cloud," Umber agreed.
"But we're different colors! Don't you understand?"

Cloud didn't understand. Umber's story made him sad. Cloud grew dark and rumbly; then he began to cry.

"I must go now. Good-bye, Umber," he said between his tears. Cloud drifted away from the mountain.

"Don't go! It's not my fault!" Umber shouted. "It's just the way it is."

Cloud's tears fell on him as rain.

Umber felt very bad. He didn't mean to make Cloud cry.
He scooted down the mountain and headed for home.

Because he was alone, Umber traveled quickly and quietly.
Soon he met some of his orange bunny friends.
Umber told them how he was chased by the purple bunnies.
And he told them about Cloud, too.

Days and nights passed. Cloud watched the battles
going on below him and cried even harder.

He still didn't understand why having different color
fur made the bunnies dislike each other so much.

"It's what's inside that counts," Cloud said
out loud, though no one was listening.

Despite the rain and flooding, the bunnies kept fighting. Then a strange thing began to happen. The plants and animals of the forest had been rained on for a very long time…

...and their colors were washing away.

Soon everything was colorless.

Of course this made it impossible to tell the orange bunnies from the purple bunnies. Since everyone's fur was without color, the bunnies couldn't figure out who they were supposed to be fighting with. Slowly, the feuding stopped.

Umber crawled up onto a rock and spoke. "We're friends today because we look the same on the outside. Yesterday we were too busy fighting to see that underneath our fur we are all alike!"

The bunnies looked at each other with lowered eyes.
They were ashamed that they had never realized this before.

Umber jumped down from
the rock and raced to the tall
mountain. He had to tell Cloud
that the bunnies finally shared
the forest in peace.

"Cloud! Cloud!" Umber
shouted when he had climbed
to the highest ledge.

Cloud was still sad and stormy.
He floated down to Umber.

"The fighting has ceased, Cloud!" Umber said joyfully. "When your tears washed away our fur colors, we couldn't remember who our enemies were. We weren't orange bunnies and purple bunnies anymore. We were the same. Bunnies one and all!"

"This is wonderful news!" Cloud exclaimed.
"My eyes were so full of tears I couldn't see anything.
I didn't know that harmony had come."

He stopped crying and the rain gave way to sunshine.
A rainbow appeared and poured color back into the forest.

Once again there were orange bunnies and purple bunnies.
But it didn't matter. The bunnies now knew that they were
all the same on the inside.

And that's
where it counts.